T.N "Lilly" W-B

Clarifying

Accompanying

Book of Poetry

1

~~~

Pain of my tears

by

T.N "Lilly" W-B

The pain of my tears I wish were fewer.

My love for you is not silent but loud.

Maybe you can't endure it but I can.

The pain of my tears I wish were fewer.

I have cried so many times because of you.

Why can't you feel the love?

Why can't you see the pain my love for you is causing?

You and I have always had that heat.
~~~

The love I have for you is all tied up.

You will never acknowledge my love.

The pain of my tears I wish were fewer.

When the night falls, I think of our love.

When the night falls, I think of our heat.

And the pain of my tears I wish were fewer.

2

~~~

Take me

by

T.N "Lilly" W-B

Take me home.

Take me in, I was following you.

Take me and my heart.

Take me and my body.

Take me and my soul.

From the passion, I have been taken.

Take me home.
~~~

Take me in from my sorrow, I could not awaken.

I'm not going to let anybody take you away from me.

Take me, I don't wish to be alone.

Take me, for the love, isn't over.

Take me and believe in me.

Take me home.

Take me in, I'm following you.

3

~~~

I want you

by

T.N "Lilly" W-B

I want you.

I want your love.

I want your soul.

I crave your mouth.

I crave your body.

I want everything you have to give.

I want everything you are.

I'll pay with my obsession to get you.

I'll pay with my life to get everything to be with you.
~~~

My reality is getting thin.

My life is going nowhere without you.

My life is spinning around like an insanity.

I keep holding on.

I keep holding on.

I want you.

I want your love.

I want your soul.

I crave your mouth.

I crave your body.

I want you.

4

~~~

Where are we now?

by

T.N "Lilly" W-B

Where are we now?

I'll give up everything just to you.

You are taking over me.

I have never needed anyone but you.

Where are we now?

You have always needed the world.
~~~

Where are we now?

Time never did change anything.

Time is a test of our troubles.

Where are we now?

It can't be over for only the test of time will tell.

Sometimes words make no sense but we speak them still.

Time will never change anything.

I will never say farewell to our love.

I will never say farewell to our faith.

I will never say farewell to our destiny.

Time never did change anything.

5

~~~

Love

by

T.N "Lilly" W-B

Love needs trust.

Trust needs to be nourished.

Love needs sex.

Sex isn't love.

I want you but I don't need you.

Can you feel the heat in me?

Sex is not sex.

Love is not love.

Love does not love.
~~~

The body needs the soul.

The soul needs to be set free.

the body needs the heart.

The heart needs to love.

The heart needs the body.

The heart is an organ.

The soul is a spirit.

Can you feel the heat in me?

I want you but I don't need you.

6

~~~

More

by

T.N "Lilly" W-B

I'm wishing on a star to see your heavenly body
because it does wonderful things to me.

I'm the luckiest by far to have you in my life.

I'm trying to understand you more and more.

The more you push me away.

The more you make me want to be with you.

The more you make me need to be with you.

I'm your prisoner, I don't want to be set free.

I'm still so in love with you.

I'm losing my mind just thinking about you
because you drive me crazy.
~~~

I love you with all my heart.

This is what your love as done to me.

Please don't set me free.

I'm the luckiest by far to have you in life.

7

~~~

Confession

by

T.N "Lilly" W-B

I'm so in love with you that I'm falling apart because I'm hiding the truth that is buried deep inside.

My heart and my soul are in one place always waiting for you despite I hate you yet I love you.

I wish you would come into my world and see what we could have because heaven is right here in the palm of my hand and it's waiting here for you.

I'm holding on to memories of minor near misses but it's all in my head.

The truth is buried deep inside that I'll carry them with me.
~~~

The truth is buried deep inside that I'll carry
them with me.

You have a piece of my heart that I'll never get
back, it's in your hands until the end of time.

8

~~~

Time

by

T.N "Lilly" W-B

Passion puts no terrible strain on me now.

Since now the times are changing.

Time makes all things possible.

Those were the best days of my life.

I never had to wonder what will take the place
of my desire
~~~

I'm trying to figure out which time to look back on.

When all it seems was wonderfully blessed.

I'm always searching myself.

I'm grateful to be myself with you.

9

~~~

Admire

by

T.N "Lilly" W-B

I admire your courage.

I admire your love for life.

I admire your helpfulness.

I admire your persistence.
~~~

I admire your that you are hardworking.

I admire your intelligence and smarts.

I admire your courage.

I admire you.

I admire your courage.

I admire you.

I have admired you from a far.

I have always admired you as a person.

10

~~~

Hate

by

T.N "Lilly" W-B

You are my first love.
~~~

You are my first hate.

You are my biggest regret.

You are my last pain.

You are my consciousness when I'm
unconscious.

You are the hate that lets me know I'm acutely
aware of your presence.

I hate that I still love you.

I hate that I still want you.

I hate you.

My hate will never fade.

You are my first love.

You are first hate.

I hate you.


~~~
~~~

Hide

by

T.N "Lilly" W-B

I came awaken from just your first kiss.

The feeling I have I won't let it out.

My body will always be yours, it's my destiny.

So many words yet I can't explain my feelings inside.

I wish it wasn't so hard for me to tell you about these feelings.

My obsession as past the mark and all I want is you.

I came awaken from your first touch.

These feelings I have I won't let it out.

Always hiding.

Always running from the desire that is calling me to you.

12

~~~

Senses

by

T.N "Lilly" W-B

If you touch me, will I lose myself?

Your warm and soft making me dizzy.

If you taste me, will I be the flavor you love?

My oral fixation is because of your taste.

If you smell me, will my scent please you?

You have awakened my senses.

If you see me, will I be pleasing to your eyes?
~~~

I've watched you changed.

If you hear me, will my voice make you come?

Come for me.

Touching you makes my desire raise.

Tasting you makes me thirsty.

Smelling you bring back memories.

Seeing you brings the most beautiful colors alive.

Hearing you is pure bliss to my ear.

All my senses are alive because of you.

13

~~~

And if there's danger, I'm not aware.

by

T.N "Lilly" W-B
~~~

And if there's danger, I'm not aware.

We kiss.

And if there's danger, I'm not aware.

We touch.

And if there's danger, I'm not aware.

We smell.

And if there's danger, I'm not aware.

We seek out each other's body.

And if there's danger, I'm not aware.

We seek out protection in each other's arms.

And if there's danger, I'm not aware.

We can elevate.

And if there's danger, I'm not aware.

We talk.


~~~
~~~

Core

by

T.N "Lilly" W-B

My core is hard.

My core is soft.

My core is full of pain.

My core runs hot.

My core runs cold.

My core is restless.

My core is priceless.

My core is unspoken.

My core is happy.

My core is sad.

My core is me.

I am my core.

15

~~~

Blood and soul

by

T.N "Lilly" W-B

My soul is my blood.

My desire is my soul's blood.

My blood keeps my soul from leaving me.

My desire is always wanting my soul.

I'm deep in my thoughts.

I'm deep in my soul.

I'm deep in my blood.

My blood is alive.

My soul is alive.

My blood and soul are dead.
~~~

~~~

Dead

by

T.N "Lilly" W-B

The day is dead.

The night is dead.

The day is grey.

The night is black.

There are no colors anymore.

My blood is red.

My blood as a color.

Dead is nothingness.

Dead is pain.

I am dead.

I am dead.
~~~

~~~

Tell me....a story

by

T.N "Lilly" W-B

Tell me a story about you in real life.

Tell me a story about who you admire.

Tell me a story about fighting fire with fire.

Tell me a story about what you desire.

Tell me a story about the blessings in your life.

Tell me a story about all the good things in your life.

Tell me a story.

Tell me a story.

Tell me a story because I love stories.

tell me a story about your first love.

Tell me a story about your first desire.

Tell me a story about who you trust the most in this world.

Tell me....a story.
~~~